Madge Eekal's
CHRISTMAS

In Loving Memory of
Ellen Violet Riley

Matador
9 Priory Business Park,
Wistow Road, Kibworth Beauchamp,
Leicestershire. LE8 0RX
Tel: 0116 279 2299
Email: books@troubador.co.uk
Web: www.troubador.co.uk/matador
Twitter: @matadorbooks

ISBN 9781788036535

British Library Cataloguing in Publication Data.
A catalogue record for this book is available from the British Library.

Printed and bound in Malta by Gutenberg Press Ltd
Typeset in 17pt Arial by Troubador Publishing Ltd, Leicester, UK

Matador is an imprint of Troubador Publishing Ltd

Madge Eekal's CHRiSTMaS

COLLEEN AND ZED JACEY

It was nearly Christmas and all the witches
were busy putting up their festive lights.
All, that is, except Madge Eekal.

"What's happened to our fairy lights?"
asked her pet dragon, Ashon.

Madge frowned. "I've tried and I've tried," she said.

"But I can't get them to work."

Ashon sighed and looked down at the town below.
"I wish we had electricity like everyone else."

"That's the answer!" Madge jumped up.
"We'll make our own electricity."

"But, Madge, it's not that easy to make electricity."

"Nonsense. I know the perfect spell.
I just need to attach these old electric lights
to my bike and tap twice – or was it three times –
with my magic wand."

Ashon groaned. Things always went wrong
when Madge used her magic wand.

"I don't believe it!" Ashon let out an excited squeal as the lights began to glow. "Pedal faster Madge! This might just work!"

But he spoke too soon…

PiNG

BANG!

The lights eXpLoded in a mass of colour.

"Right, from now on, NO more spells," Ashon said firmly.

"I suppose so." Madge nodded and pulled another bit of Christmas tree from her hair.

"Perhaps we could try something else?"

Ashon thought for a long time. "What about coloured candles?"

"It's incredible," Madge whispered as Ashon lit the last candle. "They're just as good as fairy lights."

But she spoke too soon…

"Ahhhhhhh…" Madge screamed.
"The branch … the tree ….
the curtains … the house.
They're on **FIRE!**"

"Don't worry! Don't panic!"
Ashon grabbed a bucket and
started filling it with water.
"I'll put the fire out."

"That's it! I've had enough.
I don't care what you say Ashon.
I'm using my magic wand."

Ashon looked at Madge's singed hair and soggy dress
and decided not to argue.
"Okay but we should start with small things
like egg cups, fruit or shoelaces."

"Abara-ca…" Madge paused. "What's the next bit?"

"d-a-b-r-a," Ashon said slowly.

"Oh, yes!" Madge waved her wand. "Abara-ca-pocus."

Ashon moaned. Why could Madge never
remember the correct words?

"Bother.

Not a single light."

Madge sighed and reached for her wand.
"Not to worry. I'll try a different spell."

"NO!" said Ashon quickly. He sorted through the
things the spell had made. "These are really pretty.
See how they sparkle. Why don't we use them to
decorate the tree?"

"You're right." Madge smiled as she arranged
the last glittering shoelace on the tree.
"These do look good."

Ashon laughed and pointed at the window.
"Perhaps the other witches think so too."

He was right.
The next time they went to town everyone
had shiny fruit, sparkling egg cups and
glittering shoelaces decorating their trees."

"This is wonderful."
Madge skipped all the way home.

"And look…"

She pointed at their tree.
"The fairy lights have started working again!"

THe ENd